W9-ANU-957

# CHAMPION ROSE
### by L.E. Williams

Illustrations by
## Bill Dodge

Spot Illustrations by
## Rich Grote

MAGIC ATTIC PRESS

Published by Magic Attic Press.

Copyright ©1999 by MAGIC ATTIC PRESS

For more information contact:
Book Editor, Magic Attic Press, 866 Spring Street,
Westbrook, ME 04092-3808

First Edition
Printed in the United States of America
1 2 3 4 5 6 7 8 9 10

Magic Attic Club® is a registered trademark.

Christine E. Taylor, Publisher
Cindy Lawhorn, Art Director
Debra DeForte, Managing Editor

Edited by Judit Bodnar
Designed by Cindy Lawhorn

Williams, L.E.
Champion Rose / by L.E. Williams
Illustrations by Bill Dodge, spot illustrations by Rich Grote
(Magic Attic Club)
Summary: Rose finds herself the captain of the Wildcats soccer team. Everyone expects
her to lead the team to victory and the State Championship—they've even nicknamed her
"Champ"—but no one on the team is taking the game seriously. Can Rose lead them to
victory—or will the team be more interested in having fun?
ISBN 1-57513-147-1 (hardback)  ISBN 1-57513-146-3 (paperback)
ISBN 1-57513-148-X (library edition hardback)

Lbrary of Congress Cataloging in Publication Data is on file at the Library of Congress

As members of the
MAGIC ATTIC CLUB,
we promise to
be best friends,
share all of our adventures in the attic,
use our imaginations,
have lots of fun together,
and remember—the real magic is in us.

*Alison*     *Keisha*

*Heather*     *Megan*

*Rose*

# Table of Contents

*Chapter 1*

Snowball Fight

9

*Chapter 2*

Saying You're Sorry

17

*Chapter 3*

The Wildcats

25

*Chapter 4*

Captain Rose

33

Chapter 5
C-H-A-M-P
41

Chapter 6
Throwing in the Towel
49

Chapter 7
Lucky Thirteen
57

Chapter 8
The Winter Carnival
69

Rose's Diary Note
75

Champion Rose

# Prologue

When Alison, Heather, Keisha, and Megan find a
golden key buried in the snow, they have no idea that it
will change their lives forever. They discover that it
belongs to Ellie Goodwin, the owner of an old Victorian
house across the street from Alison's. Ellie, grateful when
they return the key to her, invites the girls to play in her
attic. There they find a steamer trunk filled with wonderful
outfits—party dresses, a princess gown, a ballet tutu,
cowgirl clothes, and many, many, more. The girls try on
some of the costumes and admire their reflections in a
tall, gilded mirror nearby. Suddenly they are transported
to a new time and place, embarking on the greatest
adventure of their lives.

After they return to the present and Ellie's attic,
they form the Magic Attic Club, promising to tell
each other every exciting detail of their future
adventures. Then they meet Rose Hopkins, a new
girl at school, and invite her to join the club and
share their amazing secret.

# Chapter
# One

# SNOWBALL FIGHT

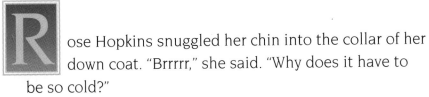

ose Hopkins snuggled her chin into the collar of her down coat. "Brrrrr," she said. "Why does it have to be so cold?"

"Because it's winter, silly," Keisha Vance said. Balancing her book bag over one shoulder, she bent down and packed a snowball with her mittens.

Rose backed up a step. She didn't trust the gleam in her friend's eyes. "Don't you dare throw that at me," she warned with a grin. "Or—"

Keisha moved forward. "Or what?" she said, her brown eyes twinkling with mischief.

"Or—or you'll be sorry?"

Heather Hardin and Megan Ryder laughed. "You should know better than to tempt Keisha with a half-threat like that," Heather said.

Keisha took careful aim and lightly tossed the snowball so it broke into wet clumps on Rose's bare head.

Rose shrieked, shaking it off like a dog shaking off water. The cold stuff worked its way under her shirt anyhow, sending shivers along her back. This meant war! She scooped up a handful of snow, compressing it into a nice round ball.

Alison McCann pulled Megan and Heather aside. "Unless we all want to be covered with snow, we'd better get out of the way," she warned. From the sidelines, the three girls cheered and clapped while Rose and Keisha pelted each other until they were both as white as the ground under their boots.

Finally, Keisha held up her hands in defeat. "I give up. No more, please."

Rose raised her fists in triumph. "I told you you'd be sorry."

Megan sneezed, then rolled her eyes in mock disgust. "You two look like Abominable Snowgirls." Heather and

Alison giggled.

Rose put on a puzzled expression. "Impossible!" she said. "How could we look like something we can hardly even pronounce?" She and Keisha glanced at each other. As if they could read each other's minds, they nodded and filled their arms with snow, then turned and charged their friends.

The five girls ran down the slick sidewalk, laughing and shouting all the way to the corner.

"Yoo-hoo!" a woman's voice called out. "Girls, come here for a minute."

Rose turned toward the house on their left. The girls passed Mrs. Lippman's house every day on their way home from school, but this was the first time the older woman had done more than wave and smile at them when they walked by. Rose brushed snow off her jacket as she and her friends walked up the cleared walkway to Mrs. Lippman's front door.

"Thank you, girls," Mrs. Lippman said with a smile. She had only a thick sweater to protect her from the cold. One foot was on the front step, but the other one was still safe on the other side of the threshold.

"Hi," the girls said, practically in unison. They had to laugh at that. It seemed that the more they hung around together, the more they said the same words at the same time or had the same ideas about things.

Mrs. Lippman lowered her voice as if she were telling them a secret. "As you know, I'm in charge of the neighborhood crime stoppers association."

The girls looked questioningly at one another.

"I didn't know—" Rose began, but Mrs. Lippman went on without pause.

"Well, we just had our weekly meeting, and we thought it would be fun to have a winter carnival. I was wondering, would you girls like to be in charge of organizing the games for the younger children?"

"You mean we can have sledding races or something?" Keisha asked.

"Sure," Mrs. Lippman said. "As long as it's safe, of course."

"Of course," Megan agreed, rubbing her nose.

"How about a leaning tower of snow contest?" Rose suggested. "The winner would be whoever could build the tallest tower that leans the most without falling over."

Heather giggled. "Or how about building a fort? Snow forts are so cool."

"You mean *cold*, don't you?" Keisha said with a shiver.

Megan looked as if she were going to say something, but she only wiggled her nose and rubbed her eyes.

"Be sure to take some vitamin C, dear. It might help those sniffles," Mrs. Lippman said to her. Then she added, "I'm sure you'll all come up with excellent ideas.

I'll be in touch in a few days with more details for you."
With that, she stepped back inside the house and shut
the door.

"This is going to be such fun," Heather said, walking
backward so she could face her friends as they moved
down the path to the sidewalk.

Alison rubbed her hands together eagerly. "It'll be
awesome," she said.

Rose nodded in agreement. "What do you want to do
to get started?" she asked.

As they turned onto the sidewalk, Megan said, "First
we have to come up with a list of ideas." She pulled some
tissues out of her coat and blew her nose.

"We'll do some brainstorming," Heather agreed.

"You're so organized," Keisha said, looking at Megan.
"Why don't you write down our ideas so we don't forget
them?"

With a smile, Megan stuffed the tissues back into her
pocket and dug a pad of paper and a pen from her book
bag. "Let's think up some neat
activities for this carnival. Then
you can all come over to my
house this afternoon so we can
plan everything," she said.

Rose clapped her mittens
together. She couldn't help giggling.

"I know! How about holding an ugliest snowman contest? Whichever kid makes the ugliest snowman—"

"Or snowwoman," Alison interrupted.

"Or snowkid," Rose said, giggling. "Anyhow, the prize could be that the winner gets ten pounds of carrots and…and gets to take the snowperson home."

The girls laughed, except for Megan, who just shrugged. "I don't think Mrs. Lippman had silly games like that in mind," she said.

The laughter faded away.

"Why not?" Rose asked. "Kids like silly stuff. We could even have a burying contest, like people do at the beach. Kids can bury each other, and the first kid to break loose wins."

"Mrs. Lippman said to have safe games," Megan said. "Everyone will get pneumonia if we do a stunt like that."

"I'm just trying to make this a little more fun. We don't want a totally boring carnival," Rose countered.

"Are you saying I'll make it boring?" Megan demanded, trying to hold back another sneeze.

"No," Rose protested. "I'm sorry, but—"

"You don't sound sorry," Megan interrupted hotly. With that she stomped off, her winter boots leaving deep waffle marks on the snow.

Rose bit her lip.

"Wow, I can't believe she blew up like that,"

Heather said.

Alison shook her head. "It must be her cold. She always gets cranky when she has one."

"Don't worry about it," Keisha said, putting her arm across Rose's shoulders. "She'll get over it."

Rose tried to smile, but only half her mouth worked. It was like the other half was frozen.

"Come on," Heather said. "Let's go plan this carnival."

"I—I have to go home," Rose said quickly. As she watched Megan march away, she just knew her friend wasn't going to calm down right away. "I promised my grandfather I'd...do something with him."

"That's too bad," Heather said. "Well, just come over when you're done." The girls walked away, following Megan's trail of footprints, leaving Rose all alone.

# Two

# SAYING YOU'RE SORRY

The warmth of the house made Rose's cheeks and ears burn. She hung her coat in the closet and took off her boots, wiggling her toes to get some circulation back into them. They felt like ten little popsicles.

In the living room, Rose heard Cheyenne chants coming from her grandfather's room. She didn't want to disturb him and she didn't want him asking her questions about her day, so she tiptoed upstairs to her room.

She grabbed her brush from the top drawer of her

dresser and sat at the edge of her bed. Slowly she pulled the bristles through her long black hair. She wasn't sure why, but even when she had to tug at tangles, brushing her hair in the quiet of her room always calmed her down and gave her time to think.

After fifty strokes, she tossed the brush on the bed. "It's no good," she said aloud.

Then she turned to her cockatiel. "What am I going to do, Little Squawk? Megan is really mad at me."

Little Squawk tilted his bright head and stared at her for a second, then went back to grooming his feathers.

"It's not like I did anything wrong," Rose continued. "I was only trying to have fun. What's wrong with having an ugliest snowman contest anyway? It's not dangerous or anything. Maybe the burying idea wasn't so great, but we were supposed to be brainstorming."

Little Squawk jumped down from his perch and waddled over to his seed tray. He put one foot on the edge, cocked his head, and knocked the tray over. Seeds scattered all over the newspapers at the bottom of his cage.

Rose sighed, barely noticing the mess she'd have to

clean up later. "Sometimes Megan can be so…so serious," she went on. "I mean, I like her. I just don't know why she got so angry. Maybe it was just because of her cold."

At this, the yellow bird tilted his head and chirped loudly.

Rose couldn't help smiling. "We should have called you Big Squawk!"

The bird bobbed his head again, then scratched among the seeds as though he were looking for the perfect one.

Rose looked at him and shook her head. "You know what?" Little Squawk ignored her. "You're no help at all."

Rose stood up, stretched, and went downstairs. Maybe a snack would make her feel better.

In the kitchen, she rustled around in the refrigerator till she came up with the last blueberry yogurt. She took the smallest spoon she could find and settled in a chair at the table. She swirled the berries to the top of the container, then started on the creamy snack, eating as slowly as she could.

Her grandfather appeared in the doorway. "That looks good," he said. "Is there any left for me?"

"Only raspberry, but the seeds get stuck in your teeth." Rose hesitated, then asked, "Do you want this one? I just started it."

Her grandfather patted her on the shoulder as he made his way to the refrigerator. "No, thank you, Little Flower, I like to pick raspberry seeds out of my teeth."

Rose giggled. Sometimes her grandfather sat for hours, staring into the fire with a toothpick in his fingers. But he usually didn't pick his teeth. Instead, he'd tell the family Cheyenne stories from long ago or teach her new words in their ancestral language.

Grandfather sat down across from Rose, stirring his yogurt with a large soup spoon. He didn't say anything until his container was half empty. "How was your day?"

he finally asked, not looking at her.

"Fine." Rose squirmed on her chair. Her grandfather could always tell when something was bothering her.

"Where are your friends? You spend most of your afternoons with them."

Rose waved her spoon. "Oh, they're over at Megan's, I think."

"Mmmm," her grandfather said, his mouth full of yogurt.

The only way Rose could avoid this questioning would be to get up and leave. But she couldn't be that rude.

"Pretty snow," he went on, nodding toward the window.

"Yes," Rose agreed, looking outside. The wind had pushed light drifts of snow onto the windowsill, creating pale gray shadows on the glass where they pressed against the panes. It looked as pretty as a greeting card. Or an "I'm sorry" card.

"Oh, Grandfather," Rose burst out. "Megan's mad at me for nothing."

Her grandfather sat back in his chair, as if he had been waiting for this news. "For nothing? That doesn't sound like any of your friends."

"But it's true," she insisted. Quickly she told him what had happened on the walk home from school. "I told her I was sorry."

Her grandfather nodded. "I'm sure you did. Did you mean it?"

"Of course I—well, of course. Why would I say it if I didn't mean it?"

With a shrug, the old man stood up and threw out his yogurt container. "I was just asking."

Rose stared out the window as her grandfather left the kitchen. Of course she'd meant it when she apologized to Megan. Didn't she?

With a sigh, she reached for the phone and punched in Megan's number.

Megan's aunt answered.

"Hi, Ms. Wyndham, is Megan there? This is Rose," she said politely.

"She sure is, Rose. Hold on while I go get her."

Rose tapped her foot nervously. Maybe she hadn't sounded very sorry. Maybe she hadn't really felt as sorry as she could have.

"Rose?" Megan's aunt said. "Megan is rather busy right now. She said to tell you she's working on something very important." She paused. "Sorry about that."

Rose felt a lump form in her throat. "Oh, sure, I understand," she said quickly. She said good-bye, then hung up.

She slouched over the kitchen table. How was she supposed to apologize and mean it if Megan wouldn't even come to the phone? If Megan was that angry with her...the lump in her throat grew bigger.

Rose thought about her friends. The five girls called themselves the Magic Attic Club because of the adventures they had in their neighbor Ellie Goodwin's attic. Rose was the newest member. Since she had become a part of the group, she got to dress up and join in the wonderful adventures in all sorts of times and places. Still, sometimes she still felt a bit like an outsider. If only she could talk to someone who knew the girls better.

That was it! She got up and stuffed herself into her winter gear, calling to her grandfather that she'd be back for dinner.

Outside, she walked carefully, but quickly, on the slippery snow to Ellie's house. Ellie had known Megan longer than Rose had. Maybe she would have some good advice.

Chapter
## Three

# THE WILDCATS

Most people didn't bother shoveling till it stopped snowing, so Rose wasn't surprised to find the steps of Ellie's Victorian house slick and white. She slowed down as she climbed the stairs, then slid across the wide roofed porch. It was a wonderful place to sit in the summer and watch the birds in Ellie's birdbath, but in winter it looked rather sad and lonely. This fits my mood perfectly, Rose thought as she rang the doorbell.

There was no answer. She was just about to leave when the door swung open.

Ellie stood in the doorway, a thick book in one hand, her other hand pressed against her heart. Her usually pink face looked pale and her eyes were wide.

"Are you okay?" Rose asked, startled by her friend's appearance.

"You just gave me a fright," Ellie said.

"I frightened you? How?"

Ellie laughed and beckoned Rose inside. "Come out of the cold," she said, "and I'll tell you all about it."

Puzzled, Rose kicked off her boots and followed Ellie into the entry hall. She took a deep breath and sighed happily. The scent of chocolate and cinnamon filled the air.

"Are you sure you're all right?" Rose asked.

"Yes, yes, I'm fine," Ellie exclaimed. She held up her book as she led Rose into the sitting room, which doubled as a library. "I'm reading a terrific suspense novel.

The doorbell just startled me, that's all." The older woman laughed at her own foolishness.

Rose laughed with her. "You looked like you'd seen a ghost," she admitted.

Ellie sat down in a large chair and pulled an afghan over her legs. She waved Rose to the other chair. "Now, what did you come to see me about in the midst of a snowstorm?"

"I don't want to interrupt your reading," Rose protested, half hoping Ellie would say that was okay.

But Ellie said, "I am just at the end of a very exciting chapter. Why don't you let me finish it, and then we'll have some hot cocoa?"

"With cinnamon?" Rose asked.

Ellie laughed. "You have a good nose, dear. Yes, with cinnamon."

"Okay," Rose agreed. "How about if I just go up to the attic until you're done?"

"What a fine idea," Ellie said, opening her book.

Rose walked softly out of the room and back into the entry hall. Off to one side stood a small table, on top of which sat a silver box. She admired the design on the lid as she lifted the latch to retrieve the attic key. The gold key felt warm, as though someone had just taken it out of a fur-lined pocket and handed it to her.

With light steps, Rose ran up one flight of stairs. The

door to the attic unlocked with a solid click. She loved the smell that greeted her as she climbed the last set of steps. It was a smell of old things, mysterious and exciting. She never knew what she'd find up there.

Even though it was snowing outside, enough light came in through the attic windows so she really didn't need to turn on the overhead lamp. The gray winter light was just a little dim, but the gloomy atmosphere fit her mood better anyway, she decided.

As usual, Rose headed right for the steamer trunk. It was always full of beautiful costumes, and she and her friends loved to try them on. It was so much fun to dig through the piles of soft fabric, never knowing what unusual and interesting costumes they would find.

But this time, she didn't even have to move any of the clothes to find what she wanted. "Cool," she said out loud as she fingered the outfit that was neatly folded on top of the pile. It was as though someone had just ironed it and placed it there.

Rose knew what it was even before she picked it up: a soccer uniform. After all, soccer was her favorite sport. She held the brightly colored shirt up to her shoulders. The green and blue and white pattern was so bright that it practically glowed. And a big fat number 5 filled the center of the shirt. It looked as if it had been made just for her.

Rose tried on the uniform. It fit perfectly. She pulled on a pair of high, white socks, tucked the shin guards inside them, then slipped her feet into the cleats. They looked brand new. Lacing them tightly, she smiled to herself. Soccer was so great. Everyone worked as a team, and she loved the running, especially after sitting in school all day or working for hours at her computer. Even better, no one ever tried to boss her around and tell her to be more serious. It was just a game, and everyone had a good time—not like planning the winter carnival.

Rose shook her head and stood up. She vowed that for a little while she wouldn't think about how mad Megan was. She hopped on her toes and did a couple of jumping jacks, pretending that she was warming up for a game. All she needed was a ball.

On impulse, she opened the door of the mahogany wardrobe that stood to one side and began rummaging behind hanging coats and stacks of shoe boxes. There seemed to be nothing but clothing. Then, in a back corner, she felt something round. Bingo! She grinned as she pulled out a soccer ball. It looked brand new, too. Perfect!

Tucking the ball under her arm, she stepped over to

the mirror and struck the pose of a champion player.

Suddenly, Rose found herself in a large room, surrounded by a group of giggling girls. The smell of sloppy joes and soggy broccoli filled the air. She must be in a school cafeteria!

"You're a real ham," someone said. "Rose, you crack me up."

More giggles erupted, and Rose looked around at the crowd. They all had on the same soccer uniform as hers.

She grinned and struck a different pose. The girls clapped their approval. Then they started chanting, "We're the Wildcats! We're the champs! We're the Wildcats! We're the champs!"

"We are?" Rose asked.

A tall girl with braces and freckles scattered across her cheeks lightly punched Rose in the shoulder. "You're such a kidder," she said. "Of course we're not the champs yet, but we will be when we win the big game this afternoon!"

"Just joking—I knew that," Rose said. This was great. She actually had a soccer game to look forward to, and it seemed like her teammates were out to have a good time playing it.

Chapter

# *Four*

# CAPTAIN ROSE

As the girls moved through the lunch line, Rose found out that the tall one with the freckles was called Tower of Power—Tower for short. Rose wondered what her real name was. It's probably Abigail or Emily or something else sweet, she thought with a grin.

"Hey, Champ," a voice called.

Rose didn't turn around until she felt someone tapping her on the shoulder.

"Didn't you hear me calling you, Champ?" asked a

dark-eyed boy.

"Oh, I— " Rose began. Now she knew her own nickname, and it was a good one. She smiled. "Sorry. I guess I was just thinking about the game."

"Sure," the boy said. "I just wanted to wish you guys good luck this afternoon. We'll all be out there rooting for you."

"Thanks," Rose said.

He gave her a high five, and they moved down the line.

Rose wasn't really very hungry, but she knew that if she didn't eat, she'd be starving before the game was half over. She checked out the choices at the lunch counter, looking for something that would give her plenty of energy. Overcooked broccoli certainly didn't appeal to her. Neither did fish cakes, though usually she liked them well enough—for cafeteria food, that is. In the end, she filled her tray with a hamburger, a pickle, and a container of juice.

The lady behind the register smiled at her. "We're behind you all the way," she said. "Here's an extra treat for you girls." She plunked a dark, yummy-looking pink frosted cupcake on the tray. "We're counting

34

on our Wildcats!"

Rose laughed. Even the cafeteria workers were rooting for the soccer team. Amazing!

She sat with the other team members at a long table. A big green and blue sign on it read *"Reserved for the Wildcats."* Tower sat to her left, and a short-haired blonde with a cute, stubby nose sat across from her. Her nickname was Spider. Rose didn't think the name fit her until she heard that she was the goalie and she called the goal her web.

At Rose's right sat a girl who didn't say much. She was the only Wildcat who wasn't full of jokes and grins. She barely took two bites of her hamburger before pushing it away. She kept her head bowed most of the time and fiddled with her napkin, even though the other girls tried to get her to join in the kidding and fun.

Finally Tower said, "Come on, Gabrielle, it won't be so bad."

Spider tapped her fork against the edge of her plate. "Maybe your mom will sit so far back in the bleachers that she won't even notice."

Gabrielle didn't say anything. She just shrugged as if nothing mattered.

Rose lifted her eyebrows, wondering what the girls were talking about. And why did Gabrielle seem to be the only team member without a nickname? Not knowing

what was going on made Rose a little nervous. She hoped she'd find out before she did something to give away her secret. She knew she wouldn't be able to turn everything she said into a joke.

The chatter continued through the meal, and Rose soon relaxed again.

"Hey, how many Wildcats does it take to toast a Ram?" someone yelled from across the room. It sounded to Rose as if everyone in the cafeteria shouted "Eleven!" at the top of their voices.

She tried to hear the jokes that made the rounds, but

it was too noisy. Still, the laughter was infectious. She could hardly remember when she'd had so much fun. Everyone was so excited and happy. She couldn't stop smiling.

"I can't wait to win this game," Tower said, taking a big bite out of her cupcake.

"We're going to beat those Rams this time," Spider agreed.

Rose set her half-eaten pickle on her tray and looked at the goalie. "This time?" she repeated.

"How could you forget the way they creamed us the last time we played them?" Spider asked. Lowering her voice, she added, "Let's face it, girls—the only reason we made it into the championship game is because the Mustangs were disqualified."

Rose felt a tiny frown tug at her lips.

"But we're going to whomp them today," Tower crowed.

"We'll show them we really *are* champions," said a girl whose name Rose hadn't caught.

"But what if we lose to them again?" The words came tumbling out of Rose's mouth before she could stop herself. All her teammates set their food down and stared at her as if she'd grown a mustache.

"What did you say?" Tower asked. Then, as Rose was about to repeat her question, Tower waved her hand.

"Never mind. We all heard you. How can you be such a party pooper? Of course we're going to win this game. And you, Champ, our fearless leader, are going to lead us to victory." The rest of the team cheered.

Rose swallowed hard. "Leader?"

"You know. As in 'captain,'" Spider said. "Right?"

"Right," Rose said. "Captain." She figured she'd better not say anything more. These girls had enough team spirit to win. But how well did they play?

Of course, they couldn't be that bad if they'd made it this far, even if one of the other teams had been disqualified. They just didn't seem to be very serious about the game. No one had said a single word about what the Rams' weaknesses were, or about exactly how the Wildcats were going to beat their rivals. It looked as if they were more excited about the pep rally that was coming up after lunch, and about being able to call themselves the champions, than they were about actually playing the game.

And how did Rose end up being the captain, anyway? Somehow, being just a team member sounded like a lot more fun. Being the captain meant she had more responsibility. It meant lots of people were relying on her, when all she really wanted was to go out and play a good game.

"Hey, does anyone else want to take over and be the captain?" Rose asked.

The girls just laughed. "Very funny, Champ," one of them said.

Rose smiled weakly. She'd been only half kidding.

Well, I tried, she told herself. Anyway, being captain can't be all that bad. I'll bet it's going to be fun.

She mentally straightened her shoulders and raised her chin. She'd *make* it fun.

*Chapter*

# Five

# C-H-A-M-P

A s soon as they were finished eating, the whole team left the table as if some invisible coach had signaled them to move along.

"Let's go check out the decorations for the rally," said Spider as the group stepped into the hallway. "Last one through the gym doors is a rotten egg."

The laughing girls jostled one another as they hurried along.

Tower ran over to Rose. "Isn't this exciting? We even

get the cheerleaders to cheer for us. They've worked out some really great routines just for us Wildcats."

Rose nodded. She looked around the gym, impressed. Green, blue, and white streamers had been hung from the walls and the basketball backboards. On one wall, matching balloons were tied in bunches around a huge banner that read "Go Wildcats!" The cheerleaders were warming up at the far end of the gym, their blue and green skirts and pompons making dizzying patterns as they twirled and jumped around.

Then Rose looked at the team. They were all dancing around and wiggling like fish on a line, each one trying to jump higher and laugh louder than the next one.

She turned to Tower. "Uh, maybe I should call the team together and quiet them down. They're getting kind of rowdy, and we should be concentrating on the game."

"Oh, lighten up," Tower said with a grin. "They're just excited. They're having fun."

She's right, Rose said to herself. I don't know why I'm being such a sourpuss. You'd think somebody made me hall monitor or something.

"I'm sure everyone will settle down when we're actually out on the field," she said out loud.

"Of course," Tower agreed.

A girl nicknamed Bull who played fullback came over to join them. "The classes will be coming in soon. We'd better get behind the thingy."

"The thingy?" Rose repeated, gazing curiously around the gym.

"You know," Tower said, giving Rose a searching look. "That big sheet of paper we're going to jump through when they call our names."

Rose couldn't help grinning. "Oh, that thingy!" She twirled a make-believe mustache and winked, just to make sure Tower would think she'd been joking all along. She followed Tower and Bull and joined the rest of her teammates behind the big sheet of paper.

"I'm glad Tower is the one who has to bash through the paper," Gabrielle said, "and the rest of us only have to jump through the hole she makes."

"You bet," Spider said. "Anyone else would probably just knock the frame down and we'd have to crawl over it!" Rose laughed almost as hard as the other players at the idea of the whole soccer team crawling across the polished wood floor of the gym.

The girls peeked around the paper as classes started

to arrive and file into the bleachers. There was a lot of stamping and clapping from the audience as the cheerleaders performed one of their routines to get the crowd in the mood. Not that they needed it, Rose thought. They were already hyped up about the game.

The school principal, Mrs. Whitman, walked across the floor and stood in front of the microphone. It took a few minutes for everyone to quiet down.

"What great school spirit!" she said at last.

Shouts of "Yaaay, Wildcats!" echoed through the huge room. When the audience finally settled down again, she stepped up to the microphone and gave a short speech about how proud everyone was that the school had done so well. The students broke into more applause.

Rose and her teammates grinned and patted one another on the back in exaggerated congratulations.

Mrs. Whitman then beckoned the coach and cheerleaders over to introduce the team. Rose's ears rang from all the noise, but she had to admit that all this attention was fun.

The cheerleaders skipped into formation. "Give me a

T!" they shouted. The crowd shouted back "T!"

"Give me an O!"

"O!"

"Give me a W!"

"W!"

"Give me an E!"

"E!"

"Give me an R!"

"R!" screamed the audience.

"What does that spell?"

"TOWER!"

"Tower of what?" yelled the cheerleaders.

"TOWER OF POWER!" screamed the crowd.

With that, Tower smashed through the paper barricade. The shouting and cheering got even louder. Rose couldn't believe it. It sounded like thousands of spectators at a professional basketball game or something. She'd never seen a school with so much enthusiasm. If the Wildcats lost, she realized, the whole school would be devastated.

She didn't want to think about that, or about being the captain.

The cheerleaders continued to announce the players. Calling off Gabrielle's name took a while, but the crowd still cheered wildly. Gabrielle bowed for them and showed off her muscles, just as all the others had done.

The last person to be called was "C—H—A—M—P!"

Rose's heart pounded as she jumped through the hole in the paper, raced over to her teammates, and bowed to the crowd. She yelled just as loud as the others when the cheerleaders led everyone through the last cheer. After all that excitement, she was almost glad when the pep rally was over and it was time for the last class of the day.

As she was leaving the gym, the principal called her aside. "We know you'll knock them off their feet this afternoon, Champ," she said. "You've been a wonderful captain and we all know we can count on you."

Rose stopped in her tracks. "Uh, thanks," she said, trying to smile. She knew Mrs. Whitman was just being nice, but it felt like a load of bricks was being placed on her shoulders.

"Break a leg," Mrs. Whitman added. Then she frowned. "Or is that only for actors?" She shook her head. "I don't remember, but you know what I mean, right?"

Rose nodded. Sure she did. It meant win the game or else.

# Chapter Six

# THROWING IN THE TOWEL

ome on, let's go to math and get it over with,"
Tower said, grabbing Rose's arm. "Game or no
game, you know how Mrs. Kerney is about tardiness."

In the hall, someone called, "Down with the Rams!"
Several people hooted and pumped their fists toward the
ceiling.

Tower bowed to the fans. Rose grinned, but she felt a
little sick inside. Everyone was really counting on her to
win this game. Everywhere she looked there were posters

on the walls supporting the team. Kids were exchanging trading cards of the team members, which Tower said the art classes had made. Many people had painted their faces blue, green, and white. Even teachers were into it, giving the girls a thumbs-up as they passed.

Rose's heart sank a little more when she and Tower stepped into the math classroom. Mrs. Kerney was wearing a blue and white striped shirt and a bright green skirt with blue stripes down the sides like the team uniform shorts. She had written "GO WILDCATS!!!!!!!" on the board with colored chalk.

Rose couldn't concentrate on the lesson. She kept thinking about the afternoon's game. This was for the regional championship. If the Wildcats won—or when they won, as everyone seemed to think they would— they'd move on to the state championships, something the school had never done before. Everyone was counting on her, Rose, to lead the team to victory.

"Come on," Tower said after class, practically dragging Rose to the door. "Time to show those Rams who's the boss! Wildcats rule!" she shouted.

In the locker room, Rose was relieved to find that all the lockers had numbers on them. As she sauntered down the aisle, looking for locker number 5, she made encouraging comments to each of the girls. She hoped she sounded more confident than she felt—and that it wasn't too obvious that she had no idea where her locker was.

When she found it, the door was ajar and the padlock was open. From her duffel bag, she removed her team jacket and cap. She figured the girls would warm up in these before the game. Then she stuffed the bag inside the locker and pushed the door shut.

Her heart felt like a huge, bouncing soccer ball in her chest. She'd never felt so much pressure before a game. The other girls didn't seem to be bothered, though. They were as cheerful and chatty as they'd been in the lunchroom. One of them was balancing on a bench, pretending to be a gymnast.

Suddenly the girl jumped into the air, did a flip, and landed on her feet. The Wildcats clapped and whistled—except for Rose.

"Are you crazy?" Rose demanded. "You could have hurt yourself."

The girl just shrugged. "Come on, Champ, I do that all the time. It never bothered you before."

Rose sighed. "I just don't want you to break a leg, or your head, before the big game."

"I'm way too cool for that," the girl said, crossing her

arms and sticking one foot out. "That's why I'm called Super Cool. Oh, yeah, I'm *Super Cool!*" Then she danced her way out of the locker room.

The rest of the team watched to see what Rose would do. She just smiled thinly.

Pretty soon Rose was the only one left in the room. She sat on a bench and rested her forehead in her hands. I really don't need this, she thought. I love soccer, but being the captain for such an important game is taking the fun out of it. Especially since no one else on the team seems to be taking the game seriously at all.

She stood up and opened her locker again. A small mirror was mounted on the inside of the door. She had made her decision: She was ready to go back to Ellie's attic. She nodded firmly.

"Oh, hi, I didn't know anyone was still in here."

Rose whirled around. "Gabrielle!" she exclaimed. "You startled me."

Gabrielle gave a small smile. "Sorry. I figured everyone would be out on the field by now."

"I—I was just..." Rose's words trailed off. Just what? Leaving? Throwing in the towel? Being a quitter? She needed a second to figure out what to tell Gabrielle. She sat down on the bench, then pulled her hair into a ponytail and started to braid it.

"Why are you late?" Rose asked when she had

regained her composure.

"I had to stay after for Mrs. Parker. I still get confused about dangling participles and subjunctive cases."

Rose laughed. "I don't blame you. I have a lot of trouble keeping all that straight, too." She paused. How should she bring up the subject? "Are you excited about the game?" she began.

For a second, Gabrielle didn't say anything. "Not really," she finally admitted.

"What? You're kidding. Everyone else around here is jumping for joy. Literally," Rose said, thinking of Super

Cool's flip off the bench.

Gabrielle sat down next to Rose, sighing as she tightened the laces on her cleats. "That's because everyone else is going to play. Coach Stover will never put me in the game."

"Why not?"

She made a face. "My grades."

Rose understood that she should know all this already. "Go ahead, tell me about it, Gabrielle."

Gabrielle hesitated, then seemed to make up her mind. "Well, okay. It can't hurt anything now. You know I never was that great a soccer player. I spent a lot of time practicing—time I should have been using for my homework," she explained. "I kind of got behind in my classes, but my teachers promised not to tell my mom if I came for extra help until I got caught up. I've had to stay after school for help in English and Social Studies every day for a couple of weeks. That's why I missed all those practices lately."

Rose nodded sympathetically. She couldn't help thinking the number on Gabrielle's shirt—13—was fitting. Gabrielle seemed unlucky, all right. But what she said was, "Don't worry about it. Everyone thinks we're going to win this game, so you can play in the next one."

Gabrielle didn't look any happier. "I guess so," she said.

Rose fiddled with the elastic band at the end of her

braid, wishing Gabrielle would leave so she could use the mirror to get home.

But Gabrielle didn't show any signs of wanting to get to the soccer field. "Now my mom won't see me play," she went on. "She's leaving work early today so she can come to the game. She'll wonder why I sat on the bench the whole time."

Rose felt sorry for the girl. No wonder she had looked so sad at lunch. "What are you going to do?" she asked, as she placed her duffel bag by her locker.

Gabrielle held up her hands. "What can I do about it? After the game my mom will know the truth. She'll find out that I've been messing up. And that she lost a day's pay to see me sit on the bench."

"Will she be mad?"

"No, just disappointed, and that's tons worse."

Rose knew exactly what Gabrielle was going through. She hated it when she let her parents or her grandfather down. It made her feel terrible. Maybe she could talk to the coach and convince her to let Gabrielle play. But if she did that, she couldn't return to the attic just yet.

It only took a second to decide. She had to help Gabrielle.

Chapter

# Seven

# LUCKY THIRTEEN

R ose slammed her locker closed, and she and
Gabrielle walked down the hall to the double doors
that led to the playing field. The sky was slightly overcast,
and the cool air blew against their faces.

"At least we won't boil during the game," Rose said.

Gabrielle sighed. "Yeah, sitting on the bench is really
hot work."

Rose gave the girl a sideways glance. She sure wasn't
making Gabrielle feel any better. She'd better just keep

her mouth shut.

They joined the team for warm-ups. Rose knew that as captain, it was her job to lead the exercises. So she blew her whistle and began doing leg stretches.

The girls had just finished running their laps when a yellow bus pulled up beside the field. It sported a big banner that read "Ram 'em, Rams!"

Several people were already in the stands. "Here they are," they called out. "Eat 'em up, 'Cats! They're Cat food!"

To Rose, the Rams looked twice as tall and twice as fast as the Wildcats. Her heart sank, but nothing seemed to dampen the spirit of her teammates. They all hooted and hollered and waved to the crowd gathering in the bleachers.

When the warm-ups were finished, Rose approached Coach Stover and asked her to let Gabrielle play.

The coach listened to Rose, then frowned. "You know the rules. If anyone misses two or more practices, she sits out the next game."

"But her mother is here," Rose protested.

Coach Stover shook her head. "I'm sorry, Rose, but that's the way the soccer ball bounces. Those rules were made for a good reason. Now get out there and round up the team."

Rose motioned the girls into a huddle. As the coach

went through the final pep talk, she tried to think of a way to help Gabrielle. Maybe, if they got ahead by a big enough margin, Coach Stover would let Gabrielle play the last quarter. Of course she would, Rose decided. The coach would be so happy, she'd forgive Gabrielle for missing those practices...

The whistle blew to start the game, and Rose felt her heart race. Playing soccer was always so exciting.

For the first ten minutes, Rose just enjoyed the game. It felt great to be running up and down the field, watching every move and trying to guess which way the ball would fly.

Her teammates appeared to be enjoying the game, too. Whenever the crowd cheered, a couple of the Wildcats took deep bows before turning their attention back to the ball. At first their antics were funny. But then Rose realized that the Rams weren't fooling around like that. They had been playing hard from the first whistle. After all, this was a championship game.

Determined to grab the lead, Rose took possession of the ball and dribbled it down the field. The Rams obviously weren't expecting such a strong show from the Wildcats—at least not after all the hamming—and Rose was able to move the ball right under their noses.

As she neared the goal, she lined up for a shot. But the Rams were in position and prevented her from having

a clear kick to the goal. The only thing to do was to pass the ball. Luckily, Tower was in position.

Rose angled the ball to her teammate. Then she watched in horror as it whizzed right by Tower and into the possession of a Ram fullback, who grinned and kicked it toward midfield.

Rose couldn't believe what she had seen. Tower had been waving to someone in the stands instead of keeping her eye on the ball and making sure she was ready to receive it!

The game quickly went downhill from there. The Rams scored three goals in a row while the Wildcats just seemed to watch.

When Rose got possession of the ball again, she decided she'd better not trust any of her teammates. They wanted to win, but it didn't seem like they wanted to work for it. She'd have to win it on her own.

Once again she charged down field, fully in control of the ball. A defensive fullback took a swipe at it. Rose tapped it to the right, then pounded it right at the goal, kicking all the way from her hip down to her toes. The ball slammed into the net, just missing the outstretched fingers of the goalie.

The crowd roared. "Champ! Champ! Champ!"

Rose didn't even smile. There was no time to celebrate. The Wilcats were still two goals behind.

By halftime, Rose had made three more goals. Unfortunately, the Rams had made four more. The score was now 7 to 4, Rams.

On the sidelines, Rose put on her jacket so she wouldn't cool off too much before the second half. Then she took long chugs from her water bottle. The liquid felt great against her dry throat.

The coach gathered the team around her. She looked at Rose. "You need to share the ball more, Rose. Remember, this is a team sport."

Rose's mouth dropped open. "But— but I'm the only one who's paying any attention to the game! I passed the ball to Tower at the beginning, and she missed it because she was waving to a friend!"

Coach Stover shook her head. "That was wrong of Tower. But it doesn't diminish the fact that you hogged the ball from then on."

"She did score four times," Gabrielle said in her soft voice. "If it weren't for her, we wouldn't have any goals."

No one said anything. Some of the girls dug their toes into the ground, and they all stared at the grass.

"I'm sorry," Tower suddenly blurted out. "I know I've

been acting stupid, fooling around and stuff. I guess I'm just nervous. I always act silly when I'm nervous. I mean, this game is such a big deal to everyone, and..." Her voice trailed off.

"Same here," Spider said.

"But you want to win, don't you?" Rose asked.

"Of course we do," Super Cool said.

"Then let's play like we mean it," Rose said. "You know we're a great team. I don't know about you, but I think soccer's fun, no matter what. We can have a good time playing without all the fooling around. Let's show those Rams what we can do."

Tower nodded. "You're right," she said. "It's time to get down to business."

Rose grinned. "But we don't have to be too serious, right?"

The girls all looked at Coach Stover. "That's the spirit," she said with a broad smile.

"Okay!" Tower said, laughing with the others.

Rose stuck her arm out in front of her. Her teammates piled their hands on top of hers. "Goooo Wildcats!" they shouted in unison, their hands rising into the air.

The crowd cheered as the teams trotted back onto the field at the end of halftime.

Rose played her heart out, and all the Wildcats played

like a real team, passing and working together. By the fourth quarter the score was 6 to 7, in favor of the Rams.

Rose jogged over to the coach. "Why not let Gabrielle play now?" she asked. "There's only one quarter left. This is her last chance."

For a second, Coach Stover looked as though she might change her mind, but then she shook her head. "The game is too close," she said, "and Gabrielle isn't up on her skills because she missed so many practices." Rose had no choice but to return to the game.

With only five minutes of play remaining, the Rams took a time out. The score was tied at 8; the Wildcats needed only one more goal to win.

Panting for breath, Rose looked toward the sidelines. Gabrielle was sitting at the end of the long bench, alone. A couple of minutes earlier, Rose had seen her jumping up and down and cheering with the crowd. Her mother must have been wondering why she hadn't played at all yet.

When the whistle blew to restart the play, Rose raced for the ball. Suddenly she tripped and fell flat on her face. She rolled onto her back and grabbed her ankle, twisting her face into knots of pain. The time-out whistle blew, and Coach Stover and the referee ran over to her.

"Are you okay?" the coach asked, crouching beside her.

Rose shook her head. "I think I twisted my ankle a little. It's not too bad, but I can't play any more."

Her teammates helped her to the bench. The school nurse put an ice pack on her ankle, then she wrapped an elastic bandage around it.

"Um…what do we do now, Coach?" Rose asked, trying not to look pleased with herself.

Coach Stover frowned. "Well, I guess Gabrielle will have to play right fullback and we'll move Bull up to halfback. Super Cool, you take left forward. And Tower, you move to center."

Gabrielle leaped forward, her eyes shining. "Really?" she squeaked. "I really get to play?"

The coach nodded, her frown turning into a smile. "You're on, girl."

Gabrielle hugged Rose. "I'm sorry about your ankle."

Rose grinned. "Sure, and you look sorry, too."

Gabrielle turned and ran onto the field to join her teammates.

It was torture for Rose to sit on the sidelines and watch the last few minutes of a tied championship game. But she soon forgot herself and started jumping up and down and screaming.

"Come on Tower, pass it! Pass it! Yes! Go, Super Cool!"

Super Cool made a shot at the goal, but the goalie caught the ball and kicked it to the middle of the field. Everyone chased after it.

The Rams took possession and dribbled toward the

net. All that stood between them and the winning goal was Gabrielle and the goalie.

Rose held her breath as Gabrielle surged toward the ball. Her right foot shot out to intercept it, but she missed. She almost fell down, barely regaining her balance at the last second.

She took another swipe at the ball while the Rams player looked for someone to pass it to. This time, Gabrielle's foot connected, sending the ball soaring towards Super Cool. No one looked more surprised than Gabrielle.

Super Cool snatched the ball out of the air, dribbled it toward the goal, then passed to Tower, who kicked with all her might. The Rams' goalie dove for it. The ball glanced off her fingertips, right into the net. Score!

Rose cheered till she thought she would be hoarse for days. She couldn't believe it. Gabrielle had saved the game!

The buzzer sounded the end of the match, and the crowd and the team erupted with cheering and clapping.

Rose raced onto the field and joined in the big team hug. "We won! We won!" everyone screamed.

"Hey, what about your ankle?" Tower suddenly asked Rose.

Rose grinned. "It feels much better now, thanks."

"You didn't really hurt yourself, did you?" Spider asked.

"I thought I did," Rose answered, laughing.

Gabrielle threw her arms around her. "Thank you so much."

"We should all be thanking you!" Rose said. "You saved the game, Lucky."

Gabrielle looked confused. "Lucky?" she repeated.

Rose grinned. "Sure. That's your new nickname—Lucky Thirteen!"

The Wildcats shouted their approval.

Students, teachers, and parents crowded the field, congratulating Coach Stover and the team, and hugging everyone within reach.

Tucking a ball under her arm, Rose quickly excused herself and trotted inside to the locker room. With everyone still outside celebrating, the room was cool and quiet. She unwound the bandage and rolled it up, placing it on the coach's desk. Then she opened her locker, stuffed the team jacket and cap in her duffel bag, and looked into the little mirror. She smiled.

Champ. She liked that nickname.

# THE WINTER
# CARNIVAL

Rose, still smiling, was back in Ellie's attic. She put the ball back in the wardrobe, then sat down and took off her soccer shoes. They still looked new, though they were dirty and a bit scuffed up now.

She changed back into her winter clothes, leaving the soccer uniform neatly folded, just as she had found it. She bolted downstairs and returned the key to its silver box.

When she peeked into the library, she saw that Ellie

had fallen asleep in her chair, the open book across her lap.

Rose went to the kitchen and found a slip of paper and a pencil on the counter. She wrote Ellie a quick note, telling her she'd come back again soon. With that, she piled on her coat and scarf and boots, then trudged out into the still falling snow.

Instead of going home, she headed for Megan's house. She hoped everyone was still there planning the carnival. She wanted to help, but first she had something to say to Megan.

She was covered with a light, powdery dusting by the time she got to her friend's house. Megan's aunt answered the door. Her hands were stained a strange blue color.

Rose removed her coat and boots, wrinkling her nose. "What's that smell?"

Ms. Wyndham smiled. "I painted an old chair from the basement." She waved her hands. "Now I'm trying to get the paint off with turpentine. The girls are in Megan's room. Why don't you go up and join them?"

"Thanks," Rose said.

She climbed the stairs two

at a time. She knocked on the closed door. Megan
opened it.

"May I come in?" Rose said with a shy smile. "I have
something to tell you."

Megan let her in, and Alison, Keisha, and Heather all
looked glad to see her.

Rose turned to Megan, who had sat down on her bed.
"I'm really sorry about goofing around earlier. I didn't
mean to make you feel bad."

Megan's lips turned up into a wide smile. "And I'm
sorry, too. I get way too serious sometimes. I have to

lighten up."

Rose laughed. She had heard those words before!

She sat on the edge of Megan's bed. Ginger, Megan's cat, stretched her neck and purred. Rose obligingly rubbed her throat. "So what great ideas have you come up with so far?"

The girls filled Rose in on their plans, finally deciding that a snow shoveling race, a leaning tower of snow contest, and a fort-building contest, would be perfect for the carnival.

A few days later, Mrs. Lippman hugged them all when she heard what they were planning. "I knew you girls were the perfect ones to think up the games for the little ones!" she said with delight.

"Megan kept us organized," Rose said, smiling at her friend.

"And the funny ideas were Rose's," Megan said, smiling back.

"Hey, I had a funny idea, too," Heather protested with a grin.

"We all worked together on this," Rose said. "We're a team."

The day of the carnival was sunny and bright. It had snowed the night before, leaving a thick layer of fresh

white drifts on everything. It was perfect
for snowmen, snow forts, and snowballs.

By the end of the day, the park was
trampled by so many people
that it was a soggy mess. It was a
good thing Megan had thought
to rope off one area for the last
event of the day: the fort-building
contest. Actually, it wasn't a contest
as much as just something fun to do. The girls organized
the younger children into two groups. Each group was to
construct a snow fort. The best builders would get free ice
cream cones from Paul's Ice Cream Parlour.

"Brrrr," Rose said. "I hope my team doesn't win. I'd
rather have hot chocolate than ice cream."

"But Mr. Paul donated ice cream, not hot chocolate,"
Keisha pointed out.

"And besides," Heather added, "ice cream is delish
any time of year."

When Rose blew the whistle, all the kids, including
Rose, Heather, Keisha, Alison and Megan, dove into the
new snow to build their forts. The time limit was half an
hour, so snow was flying in the mad rush.

"Hey!" Rose yelled when a pile of snow landed on her
head. "Who did that?" She spun around and found Megan
behind her, making a snowball. Rose picked up a clump

of snow, molded it firmly, and tossed it at her red-headed friend.

Megan gasped at the cold. "What did you do that for?" she asked.

"Because you threw one at me."

Suddenly the girls heard a giggle nearby. Keisha was standing with a pile of snowballs at her feet. She waggled her fingers at them. "I did it," she admitted.

Rose and Megan looked at each other and grinned.

"I think we need revenge," Megan said.

"Definitely," Rose agreed with a nod.

They dove behind a wall of the fort and quickly made a pile of snowballs. Then they started pelting Keisha and Heather, who had teamed up together.

Alison was caught in the middle. Snowballs whacked her from both sides as she screamed with laughter.

Rose's stomach hurt from laughing so hard as she aimed and fired one missile after another. The little kids around them quickly got into the action, too. Pretty soon, snowballs were whizzing through the air in all directions.

"Hey, I'm on your team," Rose said to a little boy who had just dumped a big white mound on her head.

The boy giggled and ran away.

Rose shrugged and grinned. At least everyone's having a good time, she thought, reaching back to dig out the snow before it all melted down her back.

# Diary

Dear Diary,

The Winter Carnival was totally awesome. Everyone had a great time. Actually, I think Megan, Keisha, Heather, Ali, and I had the best time of all.

The little kids thought the leaning tower of snow was fun to build. I couldn't believe Ali's brothers won! Right after they got their prize, a bag of yummy chocolate chip cookies, the tower came crashing down right on their heads. They looked so funny with that surprised look on their faces! Not to mention all that snow!

Later, the fort-building contest turned into the wildest snowball fight this neighborhood has ever seen. At least that I've ever seen. It got to the point where everyone was bashing everyone else!

Mrs. Lippman said we worked so well together that she wants us to be in charge of the kids activities for the Summer Carnival they're planning. I already have some ideas for games. How about seeing who can spit watermelon seeds into a cup the fastest? And we could have pie-throwing. And face-painting. And a raw-egg toss. And, oh well, I guess I have a few months to think up even sillier ideas.

Later,